In
CLASSICAL
mood

Hail,
Britannia

Hail, Britannia

England has a long tradition of patriotic music, which this volume of *In Classical Mood* so perfectly encapsulates. Listen to the big, stirring tunes of Sir Edward Elgar's "Pomp and Circumstance March No.1" and Eric Coates's "Knightsbridge" and let the music transport you to London. Listen, also, to the lyrical passages of Ralph Vaughan Williams's *Fantasia on Greensleeves*, Ronald Binge's *Elizabethan Serenade,* and George Butterworth's *The Banks of Green Willow* and travel around England's green and idyllic countryside, dotted with charming thatched cottages and hedge rows.

THE LISTENER'S GUIDE — WHAT THE SYMBOLS MEAN

THE COMPOSERS
Their lives... their loves.. their legacies...

THE MUSIC
Explanation... analysis... interpretation...

THE INSPIRATION
How works of genius came to be written

THE BACKGROUND
People, places, and events linked to the music

Contents

GUSTAV HOLST *1874–1934*

The Planets

JUPITER, THE BRINGER OF JOLLITY

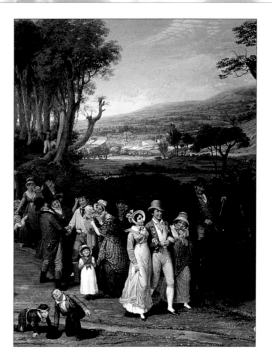

Gustav Holst's title to this piece, "Jupiter, the Bringer of Jollity," could not be more appropriate. As one of the seven movements that make up *The Planets*, this piece opens with a high-spirited whirl on the strings before the music sets off on a merry dance. Then comes a nobler and more epic theme, adding emotional depth to the piece. The inspiration for the work has its roots in Holst's fascination with astrology, but the mood also conveys his nationalistic pride.

KALEIDOSCOPE OF SOUND

"Jupiter, the Bringer of Jollity" is a brilliant kaleidoscope of orchestral sound, from the solid power of the brass instruments (horns, trumpets, trombones), to the high-pitched notes of the piccolo and the distinctive sound of the tambourine and other percussion instruments. However, it is the strings that truly succeed in bringing the whole piece together, from their exhilarating swirl of sound at the beginning of the piece to their rendering of the central Jupiter theme.

A SONG OF REMEMBRANCE

The patriotic main theme in "Jupiter, the Bringer of Jollity" evoked much emotion in listeners when it was first performed in England. As a result, words were set to its melody, with the lyrics beginning, "I vow to thee my country." The tune is often sung at solemn and official occasions, such as the Festival of Remembrance, a day for paying homage to veterans of war. In more recent years, a modern arrangement has been adopted by television broadcasters as one of the official themes for the Rugby Union World Cup.

British veterans have sung "I Vow to Thee My Country" at many Festivals of Remembrance (left).

AN UNLIKELY CANDIDATE

Gustav Holst was a shy, retiring, and rather delicate person who preferred to avoid publicity as much as possible. As a result, the enormous and unexpected success of "Jupiter" and of *The Planets* suite as a whole—which he never considered to be his best work— bewildered him. With formal recognition as a popular composer came social engagements, adoring audiences, and press coverage, none of which Holst liked. He used to say: "If nobody likes your work, you have to go on just for the sake of the work, and you are in no danger of letting the public make you repeat yourself."

Below: *The planet Jupiter. In fact, Holst's piece owes its inspiration to astrology.*

OTTO NICOLAI *1810–1849*

The Merry Wives of Windsor

OVERTURE

Shakespeare's plays have inspired many operas, including Otto Nicolai's *The Merry Wives of Windsor*, which centers on the disreputable Sir John Falstaff *(right)* and his amorous exploits in Windsor Great Park. This popular overture opens in a mood of quiet expectation, then bursts joyously to life.

AN ILLUSTRIOUS CAREER

The German composer Otto Nicolai *(left)* composed several other operas, two symphonies, and a piano concerto. He was Kapellmeister, or musical director, at the Vienna Hofoper (court opera) and became the first conductor of the Vienna Philharmonic Orchestra before his early death at thirty-nine.

KEY NOTES

Otto Nicolai is not the only composer to have been attracted to Shakespeare's comedy The Merry Wives of Windsor. Verdi's last opera, Falstaff, is based on the same play.

RALPH VAUGHAN WILLIAMS
1872–1958

Fantasia on Greensleeves

Many versions of "Greensleeves" exist. This one is an orchestral arrangement of the version from Ralph Vaughan Williams's opera *Sir John in Love*. An elfin call on the flute and soft and plaintive chords on the harp—as a minstrel might play them—magically introduce the tune itself. The middle section of the piece then brings in another old English folk tune, "Lovely Joan," before returning to "Greensleeves."

A RECURRING THEME

"Greensleeves" runs like a thread through English literature and music. For instance, Shakespeare refers to it in *The Merry Wives of Windsor* and the 17th-century diarist Samuel Pepys mentions it by the name *The Blacksmith*. In the musical world, Vaughan Williams's friend Holst brought it into his *St. Paul's Suite* for string orchestra and his *Suite No.2* for military band.

KEY NOTES

Many people are under the impression that Henry VIII (left) composed "Greensleeves." While it is quite true that the young king was a very fine musician, this tune is, in fact, almost certainly not by him. Its actual origins remain unknown.

PERCY GRAINGER *1882–1961*

Country Gardens

Percy Grainger's version of *Country Gardens* brings to mind an English morris dance, a joyous dance that was traditionally performed by men wearing costumes and bells. With this old folk tune, the composer successfully brings the listener a taste of old rural England, creating images of roaming country estates and festive cottage gardens.

FOLK TUNES

In the early years of the 20th century, many composers collected traditional folk tunes, fearing that they might one day be forgotten. In 1905, Grainger joined the English Folk Song Society and preserved hundreds of English, Welsh, and Irish folk songs and dances. In one of his finest works, *Green Bushes*, Grainger uses one of the folk tunes that George Butterworth, his contemporary, incorporates in *The Banks of Green Willow*.

AROUND THE WORLD

Percy Grainger was born near Melbourne, Australia. When he showed a talent in music, his strong-willed mother *(right)* took him to Europe. There he met the composers Grieg and Delius and soon made a name for himself as a concert pianist. He finally married and settled in the U.S., but he never forgot his homeland, and on a return visit to Melbourne *(below right)*, he founded a museum of Australian music that bears his name to this day.

COLORFUL PERSONALITY

Grainger was an intriguing, unusual character. Instead of driving or taking a train or bus to a concert that was miles away, he would sometimes actually run to it. He also believed that the musical directions used by composers should be written in their own language. This led him to abandon the Italian terms that composers had been using for centuries. For example, instead of using the word "crescendo," he would write "louder." And for him, the violin was the "fiddle," the viola was the "middle fiddle," while the cello was called the "lower fiddle."

KEY NOTES

It was Percy Grainger who originally introduced his friend Frederick Delius to the English folk song Brigg Fair. It certainly had a great influence on Delius and inspired him to write the orchestral masterpiece of the same name.

FRANK BRIDGE *1879–1941*

Sir Roger de Coverley

The sprightly old tune of *Sir Roger de Coverley* instantly calls to mind traditional merriment, inviting the listener onto the dance floor at an old English country ball. In this arrangement for string orchestra, the composer cleverly tosses the tune around, with many beguiling changes of harmony and tempo, including more than a passing reference to *Auld Lang Syne*.

THE LAST DANCE

Sir Roger de Coverley is one of the best known of all old English country dance tunes, though it may, in fact, have actually originated in Scotland as a variant of a Scottish tune, *The Maltman*. Traditionally, *Sir Roger de Coverley* was always the last dance to be played at country balls, therefore becoming widely known as "The Finishing Dance."

Frank Bridge was born in Brighton (left). *He was so attached to the area that he kept a home on the coast until his eventual death in 1941.*

BY THE SEA

The English composer Frank Bridge came from Sussex, in the south of England, and expressed his deep feeling for the area in his orchestral suite *The Sea.* Many of his other pieces convey a more general love of the changing face of the English landscape and climate. Still others are stylistically more advanced, reflecting his awareness of avant-garde trends in mainland Europe. Bridge was a fine composer in many respects and unfortunately was not deservedly recognized in his own lifetime.

TOP TEACHER

Frank Bridge *(left)* was also a fine viola player and an inspirational teacher. One of his star pupils was Benjamin Britten who remembered his former teacher fondly with a fine work, the *Variations on a Theme of Frank Bridge* for string orchestra.

KEY NOTES

Frank Bridge made several other attractive arrangements of old or traditional English songs and dance tunes. A particularly successful and popular one is his delightful treatment of Cherry Ripe.

ERIC COATES *1886–1957*

London

KNIGHTSBRIDGE

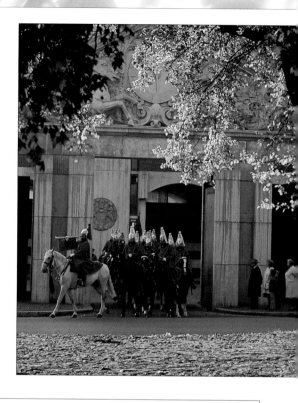

Knightsbridge has long been one of London's most exclusive and most fashionable districts. Within its elegant streets and squares lies the world-famous Harrods department store, and the Horse Guards, in all their finery *(right)*, exercise in neighboring Hyde Park. Here, Eric Coates perfectly captures this blend of cosmopolitan activity and traditional English pageantry in his celebrated orchestral march.

A HELPING HAND

One of the people who helped the young viola player Eric Coates was the eminent conductor Sir Thomas Beecham. Back in 1909, he recruited Coates to play as a founding member in his newly formed Beecham Symphony Orchestra. This certainly played a part in launching the career of the talented young musician.

LIGHT SUCCESS

Eric Coates *(right)* was one of the most gifted and successful British composers of light orchestral music. He studied at London's Royal Academy of Music with the famous viola player Lionel Tertis and played the instrument in several top orchestras before turning to composition. One of his best-known pieces, *The Dam Busters* march, was inspired by a daring World War II bomber raid.

LONDON TOWN

It was appropriate that the rousing music of the "Knightsbridge" march should be used as the signature tune for one of England's most successful radio and television programs of the 1950s, the BBC news magazine, *In Town Tonight*. Another of Coates's compositions, *By the Sleepy Lagoon*, continues to be the signature tune to the BBC radio program, *Desert Island Discs*.

For many in the 1950s, "Knightsbridge" evoked the bright lights and bustle of London's West End (left).

KEY NOTES

The "Knightsbridge" march comes from Eric Coates's London suite. The two other movements that comprise the suite are entitled: "Covent Garden" and "Westminster."

BENJAMIN BRITTEN *1913–1976*

The Young Person's Guide to the Orchestra

FINALE

The *Young Person's Guide to the Orchestra* was originally commissioned for a documentary film about the instruments of the orchestra, with parts written specifically for each section. The finale is among the most electrifying in the entire orchestral repertory. The piece starts high up in the piccolos and flutes, much like a very fast hornpipe, with the rest of the woodwind section soon joining in. The music then passes rapidly and breathlessly to the other sections of the orchestra—including strings and harp, brass, and percussion. Finally, the original theme by the composer of Britten's inspiration for the work, Henry Purcell, rises up through the orchestra in a grand, majestic wave of sound that is as invigorating as it is English.

A GOLDEN AGE

The stately theme that Benjamin Britten uses for this piece comes from the incidental, or accompanying, music that Henry Purcell *(right)* provided for a play called *Abdelazer* (also known as *The Moor's Revenge*). Purcell (1659–1695) was the finest composer of the Restoration period of English history. Coincidentally, he was also the last Englishman to compose a great opera until Benjamin Britten wrote *Peter Grimes* in 1945.

GREAT OPERAS

Britten *(right)* wrote many major orchestral pieces, choral works, string quartets, and songs. But to many, he is best known as the founding father of modern British opera. His first operatic success was *Peter Grimes*, and he followed this with a string of masterworks, including *Billy Budd*, *A Midsummer Night's Dream*, *The Turn of the Screw*, *Death in Venice*, and *Owen Wingrave*.

MUSIC WITH PICTURES

The Young Person's Guide to the Orchestra is just one of Benjamin Britten's many works to have accompanied a film. After composing pieces for the British Post Office's film unit, Britten went on to write numerous film documentary scores, the best known being *Coal Face (left)* and *Night Mail* (both in 1936).

MULTITALENTED

As well as being a talented composer, Britten was a gifted performer. As a pianist, he often accompanied his lifelong friend, tenor Peter Pears *(right, standing)*, in song recitals. Britten also composed many opera and vocal roles for Pears. In addition, Britten was recognized as an excellent conductor of both his own music and that of other great composers, ranging from Mozart to Shostakovich.

KEY NOTES

Another of Benjamin Britten's works that was specifically written with young people in mind is Let's Make an Opera, *in which the members of the audience are invited to take part in the performance.*

RONALD BINGE *1910–1979*

Elizabethan Serenade

To a gently tripping flute accompaniment, the melody takes its first fresh breath sweetly on the violins. The music creates an image of a country town in England, complete with timbered and thatched cottages, rosy-cheeked milkmaids, and gallant gentlemen. This piece was actually written at the start of Queen Elizabeth II's reign in 1952, which reveals Binge's adept talent at painting such a realistic picture of a bygone age.

LIGHT ENTERTAINMENT

Ronald Binge was a leading figure in the world of 20th-century British light music. Originally a cinema organist, he went on to compose other such charming pieces as *The Watermill*, as well as writing a good deal of music for film. He also became chief arranger for the immensely popular Mantovani Orchestra, for which he wrote *Elizabethan Serenade*.

KEY NOTES

Another of Ronald Binge's works is a concerto for alto saxophone. This is surprising in view of the fact that the saxophone is an instrument more readily associated with the world of jazz than with the concert hall.

GEORGE BUTTERWORTH
1885–1916

The Banks of Green Willow

 pastoral-sounding melody on solo clarinet, picked up by the strings, paints a perfect picture of a river or stream meandering placidly through "the banks of Green Willow" of the title. The music gathers some pace and strength, with snatches of folk song and an idyllic passage for solo violin, before returning to the opening mood. This is a portrait of the most serene English countryside.

SAD STORY

The life of George Butterworth *(right)* is one of the saddest stories in English music. Educated at Eton and Oxford, he was just reaching creative maturity as a composer when World War I began. He joined the army but was killed in action during the Battle of the Somme in 1916 at the age of thirty-one. Butterworth displayed such outstanding bravery during the fighting on the western front that he was posthumously awarded England's Military Cross. In addition, a small part of the front line trenches was also named in his honor. His tragic death makes a most painful contrast with the pastoral calm and beauty of his music.

BEST OF FRIENDS

George Butterworth struck up a close friendship with fellow composer Ralph Vaughan Williams. They shared a love of English folk song and dance and of the poetry of A.E. Housman, who wrote so eloquently about English rural life. Both composers were inspired by Housman's *A Shropshire Lad*.

Butterworth was inspired by Housman (left, inset) and the Shropshire countryside (left).

KEY NOTES

The English composer Ralph Vaughan Williams, who also saw action during World War I, dedicated his great London Symphony to the memory of his young friend and compatriot George Butterworth, who met such a tragic and untimely end in the trenches.

17

THOMAS TALLIS *c.1505–1585*

Salvator Mundi

This is church music from England's rich cultural past and is a source of great national pride. The unaccompanied voices of the choir sing *Salvator Mundi* (which translates as "Savior of the World") beneath the lofty columns, vaulted ceilings, and ornate carvings of a hallowed cathedral or abbey.

TURBULENT TIMES

Tudor composer, organist, and gentleman of the Chapel Royal, Thomas Tallis *(right)* lived through the reigns of Henry VIII, Edward VI, Queen Mary, and Elizabeth I, when Catholics and Protestants were often in conflict. In spite of the turbulence, this was a time when English choral music, epitomized by Tallis, was as splendid as any being written.

KEY NOTES

Salvator Mundi *is a* polyphonic work. This means that the voices move independently of each other rather than together, while maintaining a harmony.

SIR EDWARD ELGAR *1857–1934*

Enigma Variations

NIMROD

eginning softly on the strings, the solemn melody rises up through the orchestra to a magnificent high point before quickly subsiding again. Although "Nimrod" has come to stand for the England that Elgar loved, its opening phrase is a tribute to the slow movement of Beethoven's *Pathétique*—a work dear to Elgar's friend August Jaeger.

MUSICAL PORTRAITS

Each of Elgar's *Enigma Variations* is a musical portrait of one of his friends. This one is of the German musician August Jaeger *(left)*, who settled in England and worked for a music publisher. The title came about because Jaeger's name means "hunter" in German and "Nimrod" was a biblical hunter.

SIR HUBERT PARRY *1848–1918*

Jerusalem

"And did those feet in ancient time,
Walk upon England's mountains
green?" begins the poem by
William Blake. Sir Hubert Parry's tune
Jerusalem depicts the visionary character
of Blake's words perfectly. This is not
patriotism in the usual sense, but a poem
of protest against the scarring of the
English countryside by the "dark,
satanic" forces of industry. Written only
two years before his death, this powerful
piece is one of Parry's great contributions
to the land he wanted to protect.

A MAN OF MANY TALENTS

The English writer William Blake (1757–1827) was one of the most extraordinary
people of any time or place. He was a visionary and a mystic, expressing himself
equally well in poetry and through his paintings and drawings. He was also an
inventive craftsman who produced illustrated volumes of his own verse. Incidentally, this
poetic hymn, which is known as "Jerusalem," actually comes from a larger work called
Milton. Blake also wrote another work that he specifically titled *Jerusalem.*

PREHISTORIC MAN

The words of William Blake's much-quoted and much-sung poem "Jerusalem" are well known. Their meaning, however, is not easily understood and remains a source of great fascination and scholarly debate among many academics. Some of them believe that "dark, satanic mills" may—as well as relating to the industrial revolution—be a reference to the extraordinary 3,500-year-old neolithic monuments at Stonehenge *(above right)* on Salisbury Plain. The religious meanings in the text are rather more certain. "Those feet in ancient times" is thought to refer to the legend that Jesus, with his uncle, Joseph of Arimathea, actually visited England.

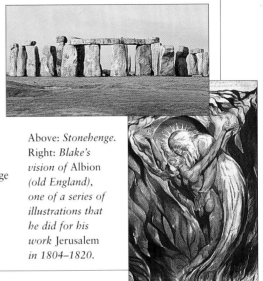

Above: *Stonehenge.*
Right: *Blake's vision of* Albion *(old England), one of a series of illustrations that he did for his work* Jerusalem *in 1804–1820.*

ADVENTUROUS ROADS

Educated at Eton and Oxford, a professor at the Royal College of Music in London, professor at Oxford University, knight, and baronet, Parry *(left)* was a rebellious figure amid the English establishment. He was also a keen sportsman and traveler, and he was a pioneer of the automobile, being one of the first people in England to be stopped for reckless driving. He held radical political views, which he passed on to, among others, Ralph Vaughan Williams.

KEY NOTES

It was Sir Hubert Parry's choral works, especially **Blest Pair of Sirens,** that established him as one of Britain's leading composers during a time when Bach and Brahms were considered the role models of music.

THOMAS ARNE *1710–1778*

Rule, Britannia!

H ere, "Rule, Britannia!" is performed exactly as it appeared in the original performance. Strings and trumpet joyously open the proceedings. A soloist then delivers each verse, with a response from the chorus. The fresh, robust, and confident flow of this piece, which has long been considered the "unofficial" English national anthem, is characteristic of the Baroque period.

FIRST PERFORMANCE

"Rule, Britannia!" is from a masque by Thomas Arne called *Alfred*, which was inspired by the great Saxon king of the same name. It was set to words by the poet James Thomson and performed on August 1, 1740 for the Prince of Wales. Around this time, the British Empire was growing quickly, under the protection of the Royal Navy, and this piece celebrates its rise to power.

LEADING COMPOSER

Arne *(left)* showed an interest in music at a young age. He even taught his sister, Susanna Maria *(right)*, who became a talented actress and singer, and his brother, Richard, to sing. His early efforts helped him to become the leading English-born composer of his day, specializing in music for the theater—operas, masques, and incidental music for plays that included Shakespeare's.

GREAT SUCCESS

In addition to being loved by the public, *Rule, Britannia!* was a big success with composers: Handel first quoted it in one of his own oratorios; Wagner wrote an overture called *Rule, Britannia!*; Beethoven used it in his *Battle Symphony* and wrote a set of variations on it; and Elgar quoted from the tune in his choral ode *The Music Makers*.

Britannia's emergence as a national figurehead dates from the rebuilding of London after the Great Fire of 1666.

KEY NOTES

The masque, of which Arne's *Alfred* is a fairly late example, was a type of stage entertainment involving poetry, music, dancing, colorful costumes, and scenery. Historical legends or mythological stories were always favorite subjects for such high-class shows.

SIR EDWARD ELGAR *1857–1934*

Pomp and Circumstance March No.1

OPUS 39

The British Empire was at its peak when Sir Edward Elgar wrote this march, completing it in 1901. The opening swagger, with a clash of cymbals and fanfares on the brass instruments, is the essence of Imperial splendor. Then, with a sudden change of mood, enters one of the most regal and elevated melodies ever written. It is all the more effective for being introduced quietly on the strings. "A tune that will knock 'em flat," as Elgar said!

A PATRIOTIC ANTHEM

The melody of "Pomp and Circumstance March No.1" was used for the *Coronation Ode* honoring Edward VII in 1902, with the words being written by A.C. Benson. The finale of the coronation gained worldwide acclaim as "Land of Hope and Glory."

THE MARCH'S POPULARITY

 Pomp and Circumstance is the work that Sir Edward Elgar is most commonly known for, with march No.1 receiving the most recognition. Here in the U.S., No.1's popularity is largely due to it being played as the graduation march at universities. In England however, Elgar's homeland, "Land of Hope and Glory" is linked closely to the Henry Wood Promenade Concerts, a fashionable series of classical concerts held at the Royal Albert Hall in London. Otherwise known as the Proms, the event was named after the conductor Sir Henry Wood *(right)* who did much to popularize them. "Land of Hope and Glory" is played on the last and most popular night of the concerts.

OLD TITLE

 Elgar took the title of this piece from the tragedy *Othello* by William Shakespeare *(right)*. "Farewell...pride, pomp and circumstance of glorious war!" declares the tragic hero of the title as he speaks out against the false heroics of the military—a view perhaps shared by Elgar?

KEY NOTES

Pomp and Circumstance is actually a title given to a set of five marches written by Elgar. Although No.1 is the best known of the series, No.4 was the wedding march for the Prince and Princess of Wales at their wedding in 1980.

Credits & Acknowledgments

PICTURE CREDITS

Cover /Title and Contents Pages/ IBC: The Image Bank/Steve Krongard; AKG London: 4(t & b); Bridgeman Art Library, London/Spink & Son Ltd, London (E.V. Kippingille: Going to the Fair): 2(r); Philip Mould Historical Portraits Ltd (English School: Henry VIII): 5(b); Private Collection: 8(t); (William Blake: Jerusalem Emanation of the Giant Albion): 21(cr); Clive House Museum, Shrewsbury (W. Williams: Morning at Coalbrookdale): 20(r); O'Shea Gallery, London (R.Morden: Prospect of London): 23(b; Phillips the Fine Art Auctioneers (Ernest Wallcousins: The Eroica): 25(r); The Elgar Foundation: 19(b); Mary Evans Picture Library: 9(t), 11(t), 17(bc), 22, 23(tl); Fine Art Photographic Library/ Haynes Fine Art (Robert Atkinson: The Rose Garden): 6; Ronald Grant Archive: 14(b); Hulton Getty: 7(b); The Image Bank: 3(br); Images Colour Library: 5(t), 15(t), 17(bl), 19(t), 21(tr); Charles Walker Collection: 18(t); Lebrecht Collection: 3(t), 7(t), 9(b), 13(tr & br), 17(t), 18(b), 21(bl), 25(l); Wolf Suschitzky: 11(b); M-Press Picture Library: 23(tr); Performing Arts Library/Clive Barda: 12-13, 24, Louis Ingi 14(b); Zefa: 16; Colin Maher: 10(r); R. Bond: 3(l).

All illustrations and symbols: John See